Jasmine

Aladdin

Starring

Circus
Owner

Rajah

Mallika

First published by Parragon in 2010

Parragon
Queen Street House
4 Queen Street
Bath, BA1 1HE, UK

ISBN 978-1-4075-8454-6
Printed in China

Jasmine the Matchmaker

Bath New York Singapore Hong Kong Cologne Delhi Melbourne

One morning, as on every morning, Jasmine and Rajah rode through the busy streets of Agrabah in their royal coach. By now, most of the merchants in the marketplace were used to seeing the princess – and even her faithful tiger – outside the palace walls.

Suddenly, the coach stopped at a large, colourful tent that was set up at the end of a road. The street, it seemed, had been blocked by a travelling show.

"Oh, how fun!" Jasmine exclaimed as she read the sign posted near the tent. "There's a circus in town! I'll have to tell Aladdin as soon as we get home. And speaking of home," she went on, "we really should be going. It's almost time for lunch."

CIRCUS
1 WEEK ONLY
2 SHOWS A DAY

Back at the palace, however, Rajah hardly touched his lunch.

"Goodness," Jasmine said to Aladdin. "This isn't like Rajah, at all."

"What do you think is wrong with him?" Aladdin asked Jasmine. Neither of them had ever seen Rajah so quiet or sullen – or not hungry! – before.

But Jasmine could only shrug. "I haven't the faintest idea," she replied.

The next morning, Jasmine got ready to go to the marketplace once again, this time with Aladdin. After the way Rajah had been acting, she naturally assumed the tiger would not want to leave the palace. But to Jasmine's surprise, he seemed more than happy to go.

They stopped in front of the circus tent, where Jasmine showed
the poster to Aladdin. "Doesn't that look fun?!" she said. "Hmm…do
you think Rajah would like to go?"

Aladdin looked at the poster, and at Rajah's dreamy eyes. "Yes,"
he told Jasmine. "I think he would like that very much!"

So that very afternoon, Jasmine, Aladdin, Rajah and Abu all went to the circus. The ring was full of exciting, marvellous acts. There were clowns, and acrobats and sword-swallowing giants. There were dogs, and horses and monkeys that could juggle and jump through hoops!

"This is wonderful!" exclaimed Jasmine. "Rajah, don't you agree?"

But instead of looking delighted, Rajah looked more solemn than ever before.

"I thought he'd be happy," Jasmine told Aladdin.

"He will," said Aladdin. "Just wait."

Shortly, the lights dimmed and the circus owner
stepped up to make an announcement. "Ladies and
gentlemen," he called, "I now present Mallika, the star
of our show!" And out walked a beautiful tigress.

Instantly, Jasmine saw Rajah's face light up. Rajah
was in love!

Before they knew it, the show was over and Mallika, the tigress, returned backstage. Rajah's face fell once again. But Jasmine had an idea.

"Let's go backstage," she suggested, "and see if we can meet her!"

They hurried out of the tent and around to the performers' cages. Mallika's was not hard to find at all.

"Rajah," said Jasmine, "meet Mallika. Mallika, this is Rajah."

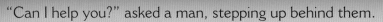

"Can I help you?" asked a man, stepping up behind them.

Jasmine turned to see the owner of the circus.

"Well...," Jasmine began, "I would love to offer Mallika a home at my palace menagerie. She would be very happy there and –"

"Your highness, please understand," the circus owner replied nervously, "Mallika is our star. Without her, there wouldn't be a circus."

Needless to say, Rajah returned to the palace miserable. Jasmine tried her very best to cheer him up.

She had the royal chef prepare his favourite meals.

She had the royal tailor sew him a brand new bed.

She even had the royal animal-keeper bring in a line of tigers to be Rajah's friends.

But nothing seemed to cheer up Rajah. Not even a little.

"Poor Rajah," Jasmine told Aladdin later that evening. "I know just how he feels. I remember when we fell in love and couldn't bear to be apart. First thing in the morning, I'm going back to the circus to talk with the circus owner. I'm sure we can work something out."

Just then, one of Jasmine's
ladies-in-waiting walked in.

"Princess Jasmine, there's a visitor
here for you," she said.

A visitor at this hour? thought
Jasmine. "Please, send them in,"
she said out loud.

Moments later, the owner of the circus walked in – with a very sad-looking Mallika.

"Pardon me, your highness," he said, solemnly, "but I have a problem. Ever since your visit to the circus, the star of my show won't eat, sleep or perform."

"I'm so sorry," began Jasmine.

But the circus owner stopped her. "It's not your fault," he told her. "It's clear to see, she's in love. And even though she's the star of my show, she's also my friend. I want her to be happy. And so I've come to give her to you."

Jasmine clasped her hands. "Oh, thank you!" she exclaimed. "Rajah will be so happy!

Before Jasmine could
even call him, Rajah ran
straight towards Mallika.

They met and gently touched noses, clearly happy to be together.

Jasmine smiled at the two tigers, but then turned to look at the circus owner. She felt bad for him. Without Mallika, he would no longer have his circus. There must be something we can do, she thought to herself. Then suddenly, she had a wonderful idea!

The very next day, the circus signs all over Agrabah were changed. The circus was moved to a park next to Jasmine's palace, and from that day on, that is where it stayed.

A royal ball was held to celebrate the grand occasion. And everyone – Jasmine and Aladdin, the circus owner, the tigers, and even monkeys – lived happily ever after!

The End